MAKE LOVE
NOT WARTS

by
Brian T Shirley

 www.trafford.com

North America & international
toll-free: 1 888 232 4444 (USA & Canada)
phone: 250 383 6864 ♦ fax: 250 383 6804 ♦ email: info@trafford.com

10 9 8 7 6 5 4 3 2 1

Special Thanks to the following people who helped or supported me in the writing of this book.

Cover Art designed by Susan Fedor

Mom, Grandma, Sean , Lori, Brennon and Landon. Dad and Sam, Robbie and Terry, Steve Hall. Rocky D, Mad Max, Yio and Marta, Dave Ugly, Tom and NO-NO, Mary Anne Cannady, Dean and Debra. Darryl Rhoades, Noonan, Scott and Trish, Jeff and Christine and The Comedy Cabana Staff., and The Incomparable Corg Pontell.

WARNING: If you are politically correct, put the book down and step away!

You can't teach an old dog new tricks,
but it's funny as hell to watch them struggle.

It's not if you win or loose, it's whether or
not you have a date after the game.

People who live in glass houses
don't have a lot of privacy.

Live, love, learn, laugh, lay, lean, levitate,.....
ah, hell, just do everything that starts with an "L"!

Life is like a wheel,.. no, life is like a platypus....
no, life is like a cranberry..no..ah, life ain't shit!

When the going gets tough, explode!

Look before you leak.

Two "B", or not Two "B",
what the hell's my room number ?

Children should be seen as they're herded.

Patience is a virtue, they also complain a lot
when they're in pain.

Money can't buy me love,
but "lust" rents out pretty cheap.

Two's company and three's a corporation.

There's no such thing as a stupid question,
just the idiot that asked it !

Early to bed, early to rise,
let's have sex till one of us dies.

Puberty and masturbation go hand in hand.

Learn to appreciate the little things in life
and maybe your wife will too.

No man is an island,
but I'd make one hell of a peninsula .

A rolling stone gathers no moss
and has really big lips.

When in doubt, shut your mouth.

A child's smile can warm your heart, until, that is,
you find out what they're smiling about.

Never run from your problems, walk slowly,
because problems can sense fear.

It's not what you've got,
it's what they think you've got.

The proof is in the pudding,
so always check your dessert for evidence.

Too many cooks make the kitchen crowded.

When death comes calling,
ask if you can take a message.

I'd rather hang over a nurse ,
than nurse a hangover.

Nothing good is free,
that's why Fiona doesn't charge.

A penny saved isn't that much money.

The Greeks were once a mighty race,
but it seems they were rear-ended.

Fools fall in love in a hurry,
it's the divorce that takes so damn long.

Sneezing is really no big deal.

The bigger they are the more they ask
if you want to dance.

It's not nice to fool mother nature,
especially during that delicate time of the month.

Love thy neighbor, just don't get caught.

If man can build it,
then woman can find it on sale somewhere.

If it walks like a duck and talks like a duck,
then let's shoot it and make some stew.

Violence is never a solution,
because violence doesn't come in liquid form.

The wilderness is really wild.

Love is like a rock,
it hurts when you hit someone with it.

The older you get the more you age.

You can take the boy out of the country, but then you have to take the country off his shoes.

If you can't be a good loser, then cheat.

Grab the bull by the horns, but never, in any circumstance, grab a horny bull.

What comes around, goes around, kind of like a bus.

One bad apple and I'm on the toilet for days.

The postman always rings twice,
while the poolboy slips in the back door.

If man can imagine it, then it must be perverted.

History often repeats itself, just to rub it in.

Monkey see, monkey do,
sometimes I wish I were a monkey.

Eat, drink, and be merry,
for tomorrow we defrost the refrigerator.

If ignorance is bliss,
then I know some people who must be ecstatic.

If God is love, then dog is evol.

Liquor before beer, where's my pants?

When love is gone there's always 1-800-LEG-SLAM.

It's not the size of the cucumber,
it's how well it goes with the salad.

The keys to a man's heart are the
batteries to his remote control.

If I have learned anything in this life,
it's when I wash my car it will rain.

Advice is free, but who wants to listen to a know-it-all.

Being crazy isn't all it's cracked up to be.

Too many asses, not enough Chapstick.

I wish the next person who comes out of the closet would shut the door behind them and lock it.

There's more to life than being employed,
like sleeping, playing with your toes,
watching your neighbors T.V.,
rolling on the ground and burping real loud.

If you can't run with the big dogs,
then try the smaller ones, their legs are shorter.

A man who is truly in touch with himself
has more than just time on his hands.

You must have been a beautiful baby,
because no one could be that ugly all their life.

Whistle while you work, unless your a hooker.

One man's trash is a yard sale.

The early bird gets the worm,
while the late bird gets the aspirin.

Wish in one hand and spit in the other,
boy I hope you wished for a towel.

Faith can move mountains,
but she doesn't do windows.

The road to Hell is paved with good intentions
and lots of hitchhikers.

If a tree falls in a forest and crushes a squirrel
when no one's around, is it still funny?

It ain't over until the fat lady falls on your head,
then it's over.

Don't count your chickens until the cows come home.

Only lead thirsty horses to water.

Two wrongs don't make a right,
but two Wongs make one hell of a #5.

They say the answer is blowing in the wind, but I
didn't think the answer would smell like old chili.

I have my own reality show, it's called "Life",
and it's on 24/7.

When in Rome, do the Romans.

Glass people shouldn't throw rocks.

Sticks and stones may break my bones,
but your an asshole!

Don't preach at people who are practicing.

People who procrastinate…..

.......ah, I'll tell you later.

Loose lips may sink ships,
but they'll always get a rise out of me.

Respect is a four letter word if you take out
"ect" (sock it to me,sock it to me,sock it to me).

Never trust people you can't throw.

Calculus is actually an ancient form of torture.

Home is a relative thing.

Shit or get out of the kitchen.

The toilet-paper doesn't fall far from the tree.

If God were a woman then we would all be born
wearing sweaters, because it's cold out there.

Time is money, and I don't have a lot of either.

The rooster came first and
the chicken was disappointed.

There's a lot to be said about
keeping your mouth shut.

People like you are the reason
they put a warning label on Preparation H.

I haven't gone green yet
because right now I'm blue.

I don't believe in talking pots or kettles

Ask not what this country can do for you,
because this county is broke!

Charity starts at home,
then she works her way down the street.

You can fool some of the people some of the time,
until you get to prison.

Money can't make you happy, but you can rent
someone who can make you to tired to be sad.

Talk is cheap, unless you are talking to a
lawyer or a therapist.

It isn't easy being green,
especially if you can't make it to the bathroom.

You can't argue with facts,
but you can point at them forcefully.

I once saw a man with no shoes,
then I realized I was at the beach.

Being open-minded doesn't mean you have
to accept stupidity.

Laughter is the best medicine,
so take two jokes and call me in the morning.

You can't take it with you, so put it on Lay-a-way.

Cheap people suck !

Where the heart travels,
the mind follows, along with the wallet.

It takes courage to be brave.

Being wrong means never having to say
" I Love You".

If money did grow on trees,
there wouldn't be a forest left on earth!

Don't bury your anger,
share it with as many people as possible.

Absence makes the heart wander.

The key to life is easy,
it's finding what lock it fits that is hard.

You can't pick your family,
but you don't have to let them drive your car.

Why do some people say " Ya know what I'm
saying" when they haven't said anything yet?

You'll never here of a rapper named
" Common Cents".

If you only put your best foot forward,
you'll never get anywhere.

Drinking doesn't solve your problems,
it only makes them real blurry.

Try to laugh once a day,
even if you have to tickle yourself.

A friend in need is really just an acquaintance.

Don't carry a grudge, pull it, it's easier.

A man who desires revenge should dig two graves,
just in case there's anyone else he's mad at.

It's the thought that counts,
so try thinking " Big Money" !

There's no shame in failing as long as your
underwear doesn't show.

Change is inevitable, that's what pockets are for.

When someone your dating says" Can't we just be friends?", ask them if you can borrow some money.

The next time someone wants you to "take one for the team", tell them your sitting the bench.

Luck is a matter of chance.

Don't overanalyze things,
unless you want to be a scientist.

Don't buy other peoples problems, rent them.

Don't bark up the wrong tree,
trees already have all the bark they can handle.

Don't let anyone get your goat,
especially if they're from West Virginia.

Never shoot the messenger,
just smack him around a little.

Don't spill the beans, I'm going to eat those.

It's easier said than done, that's why I talk a lot.

Grin and bare it!

The road less traveled usually has no potholes.

Bain, bain, I hurt my bain !

All's well that doesn't smell.

If pigs could fly the price of bacon would soar.

If you plan to fail at least you still have a plan.

Money isn't everything, it only buys everything.

To make a long story short, start in the middle.

I've seen the writing on the wall and it's graffiti.

I like a woman with big hair,
because sometimes you can hide stuff in there.

It's better to have loved and lost than to have
messed up the bed by yourself.

Fat people don't bark, they grunt.

He who lives by the sword
should move in with the pen.

Opinions stink!

Let's send all the crappy people in the world to the
same island and bomb it repeatedly.

I salute animal rights activists everywhere,
I wish they could become the animals they say
they are protecting, then everyone would be happy.

Don't look down on people,
you might have something in your nose.

Being educated don't mean
ya gots to be all fancified.

It's getting more expensive to be poor.

To err is human, to grr is animal.

If you lie down with dogs you'll get fleas,
and some weird looks from your neighbors.

If at first you don't succeed, take a break, relax.

Don't believe everything you read,
ask for some pictures and maybe a flowchart.

If you can't say anything nice,
make some kind hand gestures.

People who criticize
don't know what the hell they are talking about.

Love makes the world go around,
while "lust" tilts it on it's axis.

It's good to know what side your bread is buttered
on, otherwise you will go through a lot of napkins.

When you loan a friend money,
go ahead and erase them from your cell phone.

Camels hate straw.

May you always be downwind .

Love is like credit,
you can't get it without any interest.

When people try to put words in your mouth,
tell them your not hungry.

Once you die, that's it, no more pancakes.

If you have a short temper, give it to a midget.

If tomorrow never comes,
then why do we have calendars ?

Those that gamble on time,
are one day away from yesterdays sunshine.

There are three words that can cause a lot of
drama, and those three words are
" my baby's mama".

What doesn't kill you makes you say,
" Damn, that was close".

I can only drink as much as I can hold.

You catch more flies with honey, but I usually
just stand there and they come right to me.

Time waits for no man, but I did see him
slow down for this blonde once.

If you can't stand the heat,
then take your clothes off....slowly.

I just hope we never see any martian-americans.

You can blame Amway on the Egyptians.

The measure of a man isn't fair when it's cold.

Bad habits are easy to make, hard to break
and sometimes make your wallet ache.

Follow your dream,
but not to closely or they'll see you.

Talking louder isn't talking smarter.

Take the time to stop and smell the roses,
but don't step in the...whoops, to late.

Diamonds are a girls' best friend and the guy that got them for her isn't doing bad either.

Complaining doesn't get you anywhere, unless your on a plane.

It's easier to destroy a castle from the inside.

One hair on the head is worth two in the brush.

If your starving, can you count that as
"fasting" for religious purposes.

The more time you spend worrying, the less time
you have to enjoy life, and that bothers me.

I've never been to the peanut gallery,
but I've heard a lot about it.

If nice guys finish last,
then why do the good die young?

A man's home is his castle,
until he loses the remote, then it's his dungeon.

Where there's smoke, there's some high people.

My patience just kidnapped my attention span.

I done did my doings.

A porno movie is like an opera, only quicker.

Take your time, but leave my time alone.

Don't cry over spilled milk,
just shake you head and sigh softly.

Remember, things could always be worse,
there, that should make you fell better.

Brian T Shirley is a professional comedian who has been in the business for over fifteen years. He has performed in over thirty states in the U.S. as well as British Columbia, and Alberta, Canada. Born and raised in Marietta, Ga., he now resides in Charleston S.C.